The Mother Whale

by Edith Thacher Hurd

Illustrated by Clement Hurd

Boston Little, Brown and Company Toronto

Books in the Mother Animal Series

THE MOTHER BEAVER
THE MOTHER DEER
THE MOTHER WHALE

Second Printing
T 09/73

```
Library of Congress Cataloging in Publication Data

Hurd, Edith (Thacher) 1910-
    The mother whale.

    (Mother animal series)
    SUMMARY: Traces five years in the life of a
mother whale as she gives birth to a calf, cares for
him, mates, and finally gives birth again.
    1.  Whales--Juvenile literature.  2.  Parental
behavior in animals--Juvenile literature.  3.  Animals,
Infancy of--Juvenile literature.  [1.  Whales]
I.  Hurd, Clement, 1908-      illus. II.  Title.
QL737.C4H87       599'.53    72-10376
ISBN 0-316-38324-4
```

PRINTED IN THE UNITED STATES OF AMERICA
*Published simultaneously in Canada
by Little, Brown & Company (Canada) Limited*

The Mother Whale

On the flat blue sea there were only the white
fountains of the whales.

The mother sperm whale rocked in the long slow waves of the sea, waiting.

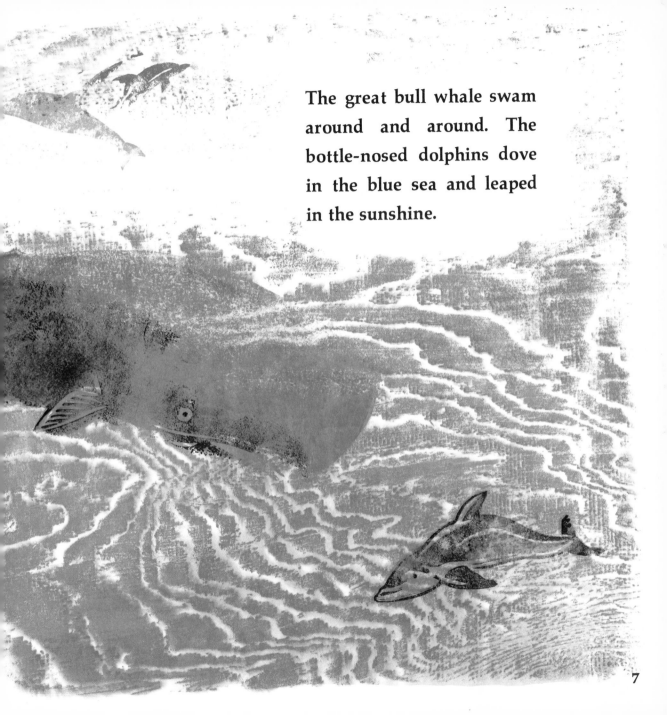

The great bull whale swam around and around. The bottle-nosed dolphins dove in the blue sea and leaped in the sunshine.

At last it was time. The mother whale held herself still, her tail moved back and forth. She balanced herself with her flippers. For one year and four months the baby whale had been curled up and growing. It was now time for it to be born.

The baby whale was born slowly, first his tail, the two black flukes curled in at the corners, just as they had been while he was growing inside his mother.

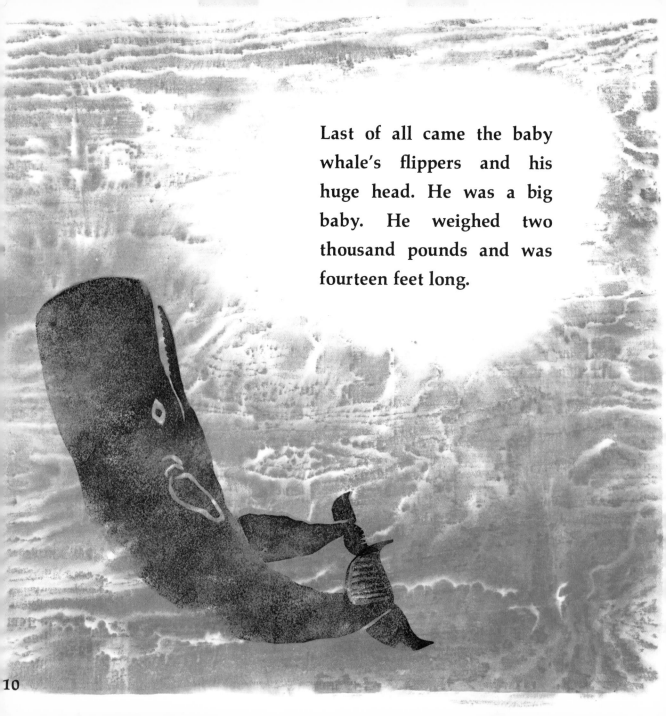

Last of all came the baby whale's flippers and his huge head. He was a big baby. He weighed two thousand pounds and was fourteen feet long.

The mother whale turned quickly. She pushed her new baby. She pushed him up, up — up to the fresh air above. The baby whale breathed his first breath. He breathed in big gulps of the new fresh air. Out through his blowhole, he breathed small white spurts of air and water.

The mother whale grunted and made singing noises as she swam close to her little new calf. He moved his tail slowly and balanced himself with his flippers. He shivered in the cold ocean water.

The bull whale swam not too close but not far away. The beautiful dolphins leaped together in the sunshine, and no hungry sharks or fast-swimming killer whales came near the baby.

The mother whale turned on her side. Her baby
nuzzled her belly. He drank her warm milk,
gallons and gallons and gallons of warm rich milk.

Then the baby whale lay still, floating in the slow waves that washed over him. Birds flew over him, screaming. But the baby whale did not hear them. He was sleeping.

The mother whale swam away from her baby because now she was hungry. She breathed in and out, in and out through her blowhole. Then she rose high in the air and dove.

The mother whale dove deep, deep, deeper. The two strong flukes of her tail moved up and down, up and down, like two huge paddles, pushing the mother whale deep down into the sea.

The mother whale swam so deep that there was no sunshine anymore, only darkness and cold. She opened her little eyes wide. She listened to the crackling and groaning and whistling noises of the many fish swimming down, deep down in the dark sea.

The mother heard the noise of something big coming toward her. Suddenly a light flashed, the light that the giant squid shoots into the darkness. The mother whale swam fast. The squid came closer and closer but the mother whale was too quick for him.

She opened her huge mouth. The light from the giant squid shone on her. Then everything was dark again and the mother whale swam up, up to the top of the sea.

Each day the baby whale grew stronger. He grew fat with blubber. He did not shiver in the cold water anymore. It was not long before he joined the other whale calves of the harem, or family, that swam with the great bull whale.

The young calves played with each other. They played with the beautiful fast dolphins. Leaping and diving together they swam in the great blue sea. Sometimes the baby whale snapped at a fish swimming close to him. But his teeth had not grown yet. He still drank milk from his mother.

Winter came and the harem swam to warmer water where flying fish leaped over the black backs of the whales. A single sea lion, swimming far from the shore, came near the harem. The big bull was not hungry so he did not swim after him. New mothers with their babies, young females and young bull whales joined the harem.

Then one day a strong young bull whale swam down from the cold waters of the north. The young bull whale was looking for a harem to claim as his own and he attacked the old bull whale.

The two whales swam toward each other. They grunted and whistled. They leaped and fell, crashing together. They slapped their strong tails against each other. They dove and rose making great waves.

But the young bull was not strong enough to take the old bull's harem away from him. The mother whales and their calves followed the old whale, just as they always had, diving and swimming together. The young bull swam away, still searching the sea for a harem that he could take for his own.

When two years had passed, the mother began to push and nudge her baby away from her. The young whale swam around and around trying to get close to the mother whale but she would not let him drink milk from her anymore.

The young whale's teeth were beginning to grow in his strong lower jaw. He swam fast, moving the two flukes of his tail. He balanced and steered himself with his flippers. He dove deep into the cold darkness where he hunted for squid and huge octopuses that lived in the caves of the sea.

The mother whale did not watch over her baby anymore. She swam slowly with the other whales for many months.

Then one day the big bull whale came close to her. The big bull whale and the mother whale swam close together. The bull touched her with his flippers. He swam fast turning on his belly, then on his back again. The mother whale watched the bull whale and swam with him.

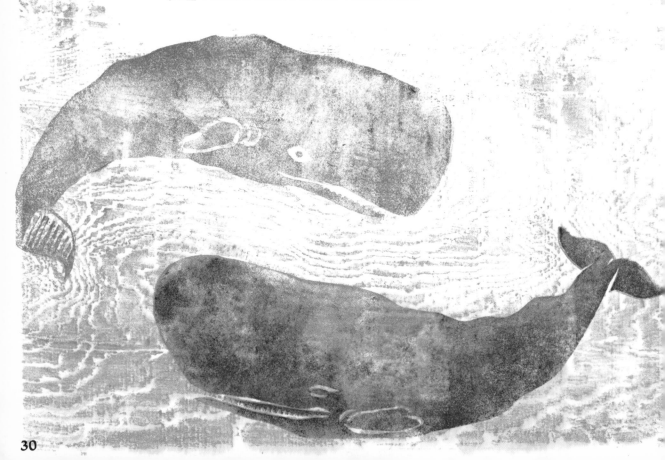

And so four years passed, four years since the little calf had been born. The mother whale and the big bull whale swam together in the blue blue sea. They swam close to each other and they mated.

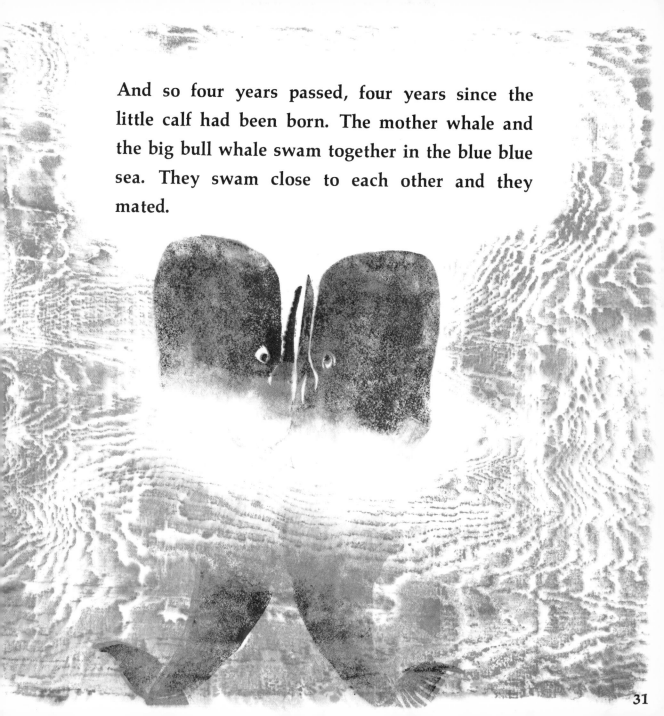

Winter and summer passed then winter again,
sixteen long months. Once more, the mother
whale lay still. The big bull swam around and
around, other female whales gathered about the
mother whale. The dolphins leaped. The sun
shone. The blue sea was quiet and a new baby was
born.